A Crabby Book

Wake Up, Crabby!

ACORN™
SCHOLASTIC INC.

For Floralei, my early morning drawing buddy.

Copyright © 2019 by Jonathan Fenske

All rights reserved. Published by Scholastic Inc., *Publishers since 1920.* SCHOLASTIC, ACORN, and associated logos are trademarks and/or registered trademarks of Scholastic Inc.

The publisher does not have any control over and does not assume any responsibility for author or third-party websites or their content.

No part of this publication may be reproduced, stored in a retrieval system, or transmitted in any form or by any means, electronic, mechanical, photocopying, recording, or otherwise, without written permission of the publisher. For information regarding permission, write to Scholastic Inc., Attention: Permissions Department, 557 Broadway, New York, NY 10012.

Library of Congress Cataloging-in-Publication Data

Names: Fenske, Jonathan, author, illustrator.
Title: Wake up, Crabby! / Jonathan Fenske.
Description: First edition. | New York, NY : Acorn/Scholastic Inc., 2019. | Series: A Crabby book ; 3 | Summary: It is late and Crabby just wants to sleep, but Plankton keeps Crabby awake with questions and chatter—until a request for a bedtime story takes an unexpected turn.
Identifiers: LCCN 2018060386| ISBN 9781338281613 (pbk. : alk. paper) | ISBN 9781338281637 (hardcover : alk. paper)
Subjects: LCSH: Crabs—Juvenile fiction. | Plankton—Juvenile fiction. | Bedtime—Juvenile fiction. | Storytelling—Juvenile fiction. | CYAC: Crabs—Fiction. | Plankton—Fiction. | Bedtime—Fiction. | Humorous stories.
Classification: LCC PZ7.F34843 Wak 2019 | DDC (E)—dc23 LC record available at https://lccn.loc.gov/2018060386

10 9 8 7 6 5 4 3 2 1   19 20 21 22 23

Printed in China   62

First edition, November 2019
Edited by Katie Carella
Book design by Maria Mercado

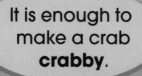

It is enough to make a crab **crabby**.

And **sleepy**.

3

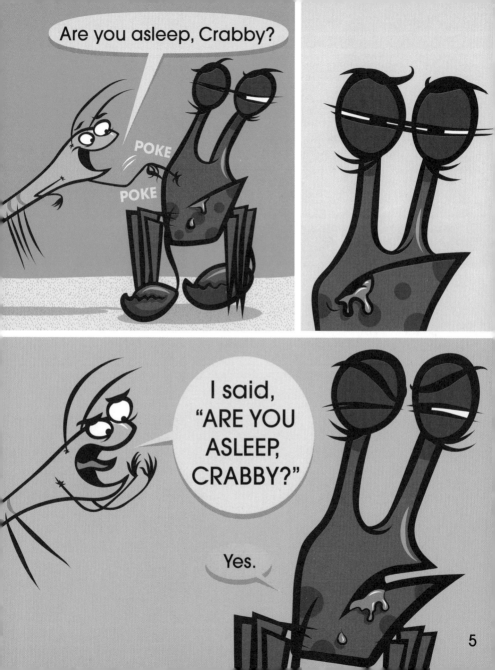

6

8

9

11

Do **you** want to take a bedtime bath?

We live in the ocean. We do not **need** baths.

Trust me. **You** need a bath.

12

Do you want to smell like a **stinky crab**?

News flash: I **am** a stinky crab.

What if it was a nice hot bubble bath?

Sea creatures should not **take** nice hot bubble baths.

Why not?

Ask Lobster.

15

17

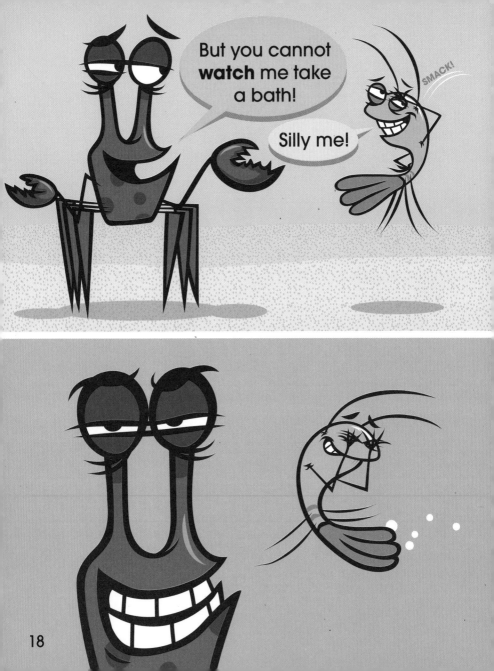

21

THE SONG

Hey, Crabby.
Will you sing me a
bedtime song?

No, Plankton.
I will **not** sing you a
bedtime song.

25

Sigh.

I guess I will not hear a bedtime song.

28

No, Plankton.
I will not tell you a
bedtime story.
But I cannot go
to sleep without a
bedtime story.
SCUTTLING
MADE EASY

Hmmm.

35

They **waved** in the waves.

Hello!

They **surfed** in the surf.

Fun!

They **sunned** in the sun.

Aaah.

They had a wonderful time together.

Woo-hoo!

37

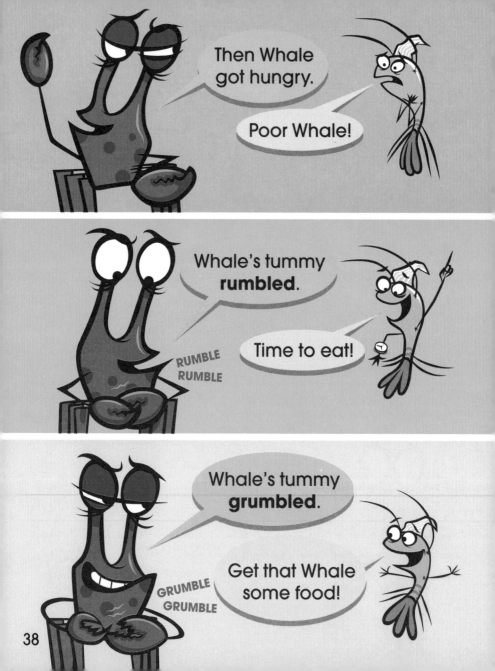

41

43

44

About the Author

Jonathan Fenske lives in South Carolina with his family. He was born in Florida near the ocean, so he knows all about life at the beach! He likes to wake up early, and he **loves** bubble baths and bedtime stories.

Jonathan is the author and illustrator of several children's books including **Barnacle Is Bored**, **Plankton Is Pushy** (a Junior Library Guild selection), and the LEGO® picture book **I'm Fun, Too!** His early reader **a Pig, a Fox, and a Box** was a Theodor Seuss Geisel Honor Book.

YOU CAN DRAW DUCKIE!

QUACK!

1. Draw a leaning figure eight.

2. Connect the circles with a line to make the body and tail.

3. Add a beak and a feather on top.

4. Erase the leftover parts of the circles.

5. Draw a circle and dot for the eye and a scribble for the wing.

6. Color in your drawing!

WHAT'S YOUR STORY?

Plankton loves to take baths with Duckie.
Do **you** like to take baths?
Would your bath have lots of bubbles or no bubbles?
What is your favorite bath toy?
Write and draw your story!